CANADA

Minnesota

Wisconsin

Michigan

Iowa

Illinois

Indiana

Ohio

Missouri

Kentucky

Arkansas

Tennessee

Mississippi

Alabama

Louisiana

New York

Pennsylvania

West
Virginia

Virginia

North
Carolina

South
Carolina

Georgia

Florida

New
Hampshire

Vermont

Maine

Massachusetts

Rhode Island

Connecticut

New Jersey

Delaware

Maryland

Washington, D.C.

N

W

E

S

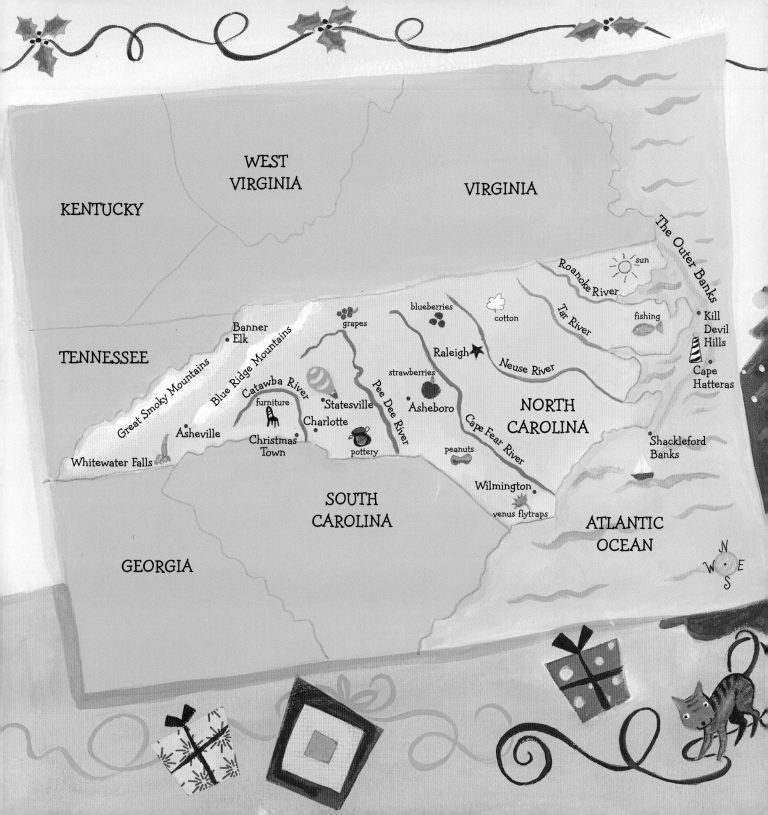

The Twelve Days of Christmas in North Carolina

written and
illustrated by
Judy Stead

STERLING

New York / London

Dear Abby,

I hope you like your Christmas present from Mom and me this year—a trip to visit us here in North Carolina! We're going to show you _all_ of it, from the mountains to the sea and lots of stuff in between.

There's so much to do we'll be lucky to get to everything on my list in only twelve days, but since Mom's flying us around from place to place in "Old Whirlygirl," we just might finish.

Christmas vacation in NC is extra special, with millions of twinkling lights and decorated trees (_your_ Christmas tree probably came from NC) and snow in the mountains and kites on the beach and so much yummy food, like my favorites: barbeque and hush puppies. So pack some mittens and flip-flops—you may need both!

See you soon!
Cousin Mike

Dear Mom and Dad,

I'm in North Carolina, and Christmas vacation is REALLY off to a flying start! Aunt Tess and her helicopter, "Old Whirlygirl," will be flying us all around the state. WOW! Mike's pet cardinal, Red, is along for the ride. As the official state bird, Red feels very important, and likes to sit on Mike's head.

Our first stop is Christmas Town, USA, a.k.a. McAdenville. Mike wasn't kidding about the lights: There are over half a million right here—Old Man Winter, Santa and Rudolph, Frosty the Snowman—all bright and twinkly! Walking through this wonderland, we stopped so that Red could eat some juicy berries from a dogwood tree. Mike says dogwood trees stay busy all year, producing the pretty state flower in spring and red berries in winter. Red ate some berries right out of my hand—he likes me!

It's only my first day, and already North Carolina is magical.

Love,
Abby

Merry Christmas, NC!

On the first day of Christmas,
my cousin gave to me . . .

a cardinal in a
dogwood tree.

Dear Mom and Dad,

Have you ever heard of a weather WORM? In the Blue Ridge Mountains, a caterpillar's black and orange "winter coat" predicts winter weather. There's even a Woolly Worm Festival in Banner Elk every October, with a race to choose the official forecaster. This winter, 1,400 woollies wiggled up tracks made of string, and Mike's woolly, Woodrow, won! His coat had lots more black stripes, which predict a cold and snowy winter. He was right—brrrrr.

Grandfather Mountain is the highest peak in the Blue Ridge Mountain range. We climbed (in Aunt Tess's four wheeler!) to the Mile-High Swinging Bridge. The wind was blowing like crazy when Mike and I walked across it—we were holding on for dear life! But the view of snow-covered peaks for miles and miles was worth a little teeth-chattering, mitten-freezing cold.

Now, we're heading over to those peaks for night skiing and hot chocolate. Mike is going to teach me some snowboarding tricks!

Love,
Abby

Grandfather Mt.

On the second day of Christmas, my cousin gave to me . . .

2 woolly worms

and a cardinal in a dogwood tree.

Hi, Mom and Dad,

Mike gave me three bear cubs today—can I keep them? Ha-ha! They scampered out of the forest and right across our hiking trail. They must have been following Mama Bear, so it's good we missed her! Mike knows everything about black bears, like how fast they can run—30 miles per hour—and how much they can weigh—600 pounds. The Great Smoky Mountains National Park is home to 1,500 black bears but we were lucky to see some because they are usually pretty shy (unless people leave food out for them—which is really asking for trouble).

We hiked to Whitewater Falls, the highest waterfalls east of the Rocky Mountains, plunging 411 feet. I knew we were getting close and that this waterfall was going to be BIG from the roaring sound of rushing water—AWESOME! Aunt Tess and Mike "collect" waterfalls and they've seen hundreds, but this is the first in my waterfall collection!

Love,
Abby

My first waterfall!

On the third day of Christmas,
my cousin gave to me . . .

3 bear cubs

2 woolly worms,
and a cardinal in a dogwood tree.

Dear Mom and Dad,

Beach day—YAY! The Outer Banks is 130 miles of barrier island beach and a total wildlife haven. At Pea Island National Wildlife Refuge we spotted a Marbled Godwit (that's a bird). Mike found tons of sand dollars, and I scored some Scotch bonnets, the state seashell.

Best of all were the baby sea turtles! Mother sea turtles come to the beach at night to lay their eggs. Park rangers take the brand-new eggs to a safe nesting area where no lights are allowed on the beach. That way the tiny turtle hatchlings can follow the light of the moon to find their home in the sea.

Tonight Aunt Tess built a bonfire on the beach and we made s'mores. Then Mike and I chased ghost crabs. They're funny little critters, running fast, sideways! They zip into sand holes when you "catch" them in your flashlight beam. Four kept running in and out of the same hole, so we named them the Four Crabs-keteers!

Love,
Abby

turtles

Turtle hatchlings head to the sea

On the fourth day of Christmas,
my cousin gave to me . . .

4 creeping crabs

3 bear cubs, **2** woolly worms,
and a cardinal in a dogwood tree.

Dear Mom and Dad,

Cape Hatteras is called "The Graveyard of the Atlantic" for good reason. Crashing currents and storms sank many a brave ship headed for shore. Some of these were warships, some were passenger ships loaded with gold and jewels, and some were pirate ships after all that loot. Just think how many gold coins are still sitting at the bottom of the ocean here!

If you want to see pirate ghosts, this is the place. The most fearsome of all was Blackbeard. With his braided beard and a burning rope stuffed under his hat so that smoke curled out around his face, he looked ferocious. If a victim refused to give up his diamond ring, Blackbeard took that ring, finger and all! When Blackbeard was finally killed in a battle with the law, his head was cut off and hung from the bowsprit, and his body was thrown overboard. To this day, people claim that his ghost swims around, glowing in the water, searching for his missing head. Sometimes, you can hear the voice of Blackbeard roaring above the waves: "Where's my head?!"

Sweet dreams!
Abby

Cape Hatteras Lighthouse

On the fifth day of Christmas,
my cousin gave to me . . .

5 golden coins

4 creeping crabs, 3 bear cubs, 2 woolly worms,
and a cardinal in a dogwood tree.

Hi, Mom and Dad,

What a sweet day this was! Did you know there's a National Gingerbread House Competition? Every Christmas at the Grove Park Inn in Asheville hundreds of people bring their sugar-coated creations for judging. Mike and I are entering next year! The gingerbread house construction rules are:

1) The house can be no taller or wider than 24 inches.

2) Every piece of the house has to be edible and unwrapped.

3) No sampling by the viewers. (Aunt Tess made up that rule when she saw Mike and me drooling over the chocolate shingles!)

From those candy castles we zipped over to "North Carolina's Castle," the Biltmore, which is absolutely THE biggest house in America. It was built for the Vanderbilt family, who moved in on Christmas Eve in 1895. It took 1,000 workers six years to complete its 250 rooms and 43 bathrooms. If you're wondering who cleaned all those bathrooms, don't worry, they had lots of help. Prince Mike says "Hi!"

Love,
Princess Abby

On the sixth day of Christmas,
my cousin gave to me . . .

6 candy
castles

5 golden coins,
4 creeping crabs, **3** bear cubs, **2** woolly worms,
and a cardinal in a dogwood tree.

Dear Mom and Dad,

Here, kitty kitty! The bobcats at the NC Zoo in Asheboro are so adorable, they don't look like they would hurt a fly, but the guide told us their favorite meal is a nice fresh rabbit they've just caught! Mike says we didn't come all the way to the zoo just to see bobcats, because they live in the wild in North Carolina, sometimes hiding in trees and watching us when we're hiking in the forest. They get their name from their short bobbed tails.

The NC Zoo was the very first American zoo designed to exhibit animals in their natural habitats, and it's still the largest, with five miles of trails that take you all the way to the North Pole, through South America, and to the grasslands of Africa in one day! Lions and tigers and giraffes (I LOVE giraffes) and rhinos and zebras and elephants and baboons and bobcats and polar bears, oh my!

Love,
Abby

On the seventh day of Christmas,
my cousin gave to me . . .

7 bobcats spying

6 candy castles, 5 golden coins,
4 creeping crabs, 3 bear cubs, 2 woolly worms,
and a cardinal in a dogwood tree.

Dear Mom and Dad,

WHOOOOSH! That's the sound of the wind on top of Kill Devil Hills, where Mike and I flew kites, pretending we were Orville and Wilbur Wright when they started designing their flying machine. It took them two years and lots of tries before they got it right, and guess what helped? A pigeon! They were having trouble figuring out how to steer when they noticed pigeons twisting and turning their wings to catch air currents. Brilliant. Finally, on December 17, 1903, they made the first powered flights. Orville (that's me) was first. He flew 120 feet in 12 seconds, but Wilbur (that's Mike) flew farther—852 feet in 59 seconds. The Age of Flight was born, and all because of a toy their dad gave them when they were kids—a little helicopter powered by a rubber band! Aunt Tess wants me to come back next summer for the Annual Wright Kite Festival to see a hundred-foot octopus dancing in the wind—unbelievable!

Over and out,
Orville (Abby)

On the eighth day of Christmas,
my cousin gave to me . . .

8 kites a-flying

7 bobcats spying, 6 candy castles, 5 golden coins,
4 creeping crabs, 3 bear cubs, 2 woolly worms,
and a cardinal in a dogwood tree.

Dear Mom and Dad,

Today, Mike gave me nine wild horses! I named them for Santa's eight reindeer plus Rudolph, because they are about deer-sized. Out here on Shackleford Banks, the old-timers say, "The horses have always been here." They are thought to be descendants of horses brought on ships by Spanish explorers 500 years ago. Shipwrecked or pushed overboard, they swam ashore and survived, roaming free on the island for centuries. Now these "Banker Ponies" are protected by law as a North Carolina treasure, so that we can come and visit them!

We pretty much know how the horses got here, but the big mystery is . . . what happened to the Lost Colony? Tonight we saw a play about it. According to legend, the English were the first settlers in the New World in 1587 on Roanoke Island. They ran out of food and their leader went back to England for supplies. When he returned three years later, all 120 settlers had vanished without a trace—all he found was the mysterious word "CROATOAN" carved on a tree.

Stay tuned,
Abby

On the ninth day of Christmas, my cousin gave to me . . .

9 colts a-grazing

8 kites a-flying, **7** bobcats spying, **6** candy castles,
5 golden coins, **4** creeping crabs, **3** bear cubs, **2** woolly worms,
and a cardinal in a dogwood tree.

Keep Off Flytraps!

Dear Mom and Dad,

I had never heard of an official "state carnivorous plant" before, but North Carolina has one and it's the Venus flytrap. Way cool! This little chomper has been cultivated all over the world but it grows in the wild only in swampy areas around Wilmington. Mike and Aunt Tess took me on the Venus Flytrap Trail so we could watch them in action. The trap doesn't close until it knows it has actually caught dinner. If it has a nice tasty fly or ant, it snaps shut and chows down. Because they are in danger of going extinct, we could only bring these wild plants home with us in our cameras.

All that chomping made us hungry, so we stopped for BBQ. Here, that's barbeque, and it does NOT mean burgers on a grill! Think slow-cooked pulled pork with hush puppies and sweet tea—I think I'm becoming a native!

Love,
Abby

oh no!

hush puppy →

On the tenth day of Christmas, my cousin gave to me . . .

10 Venus flytraps

9 colts a-grazing, 8 kites a-flying, 7 bobcats spying,
6 candy castles, 5 golden coins, 4 creeping crabs, 3 bear cubs,
2 woolly worms, and a cardinal in a dogwood tree.

Dear Mom and Dad,

SAVE THE BEES! You know how I used to be afraid of bees? Well, after today, I'll be <u>happy</u> when they buzz around me. We visited a beekeeper and saw thousands of North Carolina's state insect, the honeybee. Mike and I had to wear big hats with netting over our faces to protect us from bee stings—we looked like visitors from another planet!

Did you know we wouldn't have many strawberries or watermelons or cucumbers without honeybees? They buzz from flower to flower, carrying pollen to make fruits, vegetables, and nuts grow. They pollinate a third of the food we eat. Even huge black bears depend on tiny honeybees for their blueberry dinners. That's why we have to SAVE THE BEES! They are getting sick and deserting their hives—scientists are working hard to find out why so that they can help the bee population grow strong again. We stopped at the Honeybee Café for a real North Carolina treat of hot biscuits dripping with butter and honey. Thanks, little honeybee!

Love,
Abby

Honey

Mike from Mars!

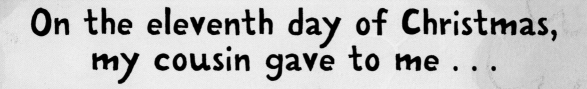

On the eleventh day of Christmas, my cousin gave to me . . .

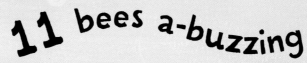

11 bees a-buzzing

10 Venus flytraps, **9** colts a-grazing,
8 kites a-flying, **7** bobcats spying, **6** candy castles,
5 golden coins, **4** creeping crabs, **3** bear cubs, **2** woolly worms,
and a cardinal in a dogwood tree.

Dear Mom and Dad,

My last day in North Carolina has been the most exciting, and definitely the most colorful! Aunt Tess is practicing her ballooning skills for Statesville's Carolina BalloonFest in October, so she took Mike and me up in her rainbow-striped hot air balloon. How can this BIG balloon rise up into the sky, even though it weighs about 800 pounds?

Going up, you inflate the pretty balloon with hot air. Going down, you have to let the air in the balloon cool off. The pilot can only control up and down; the wind does the rest. You can't be exactly sure where you'll land, so a "chaser" car follows on the ground. We started at sunrise and floated up into the most beautiful pink and gold sky, way above the treetops with land below getting smaller and smaller and smaller.

Aunt Tess and Mike made me an official "balloon-atic"! I can't wait to come back for more North Carolina adventures.

Love,
Abby

chaser car

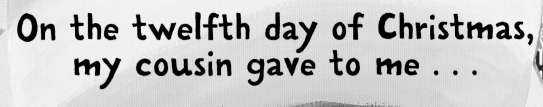

On the twelfth day of Christmas, my cousin gave to me . . .

12 balloons a-rising

11 bees a-buzzing, 10 Venus flytraps, 9 colts a-grazing,
8 kites a-flying, 7 bobcats spying, 6 candy castles, 5 golden coins,
4 creeping crabs, 3 bear cubs, 2 woolly worms,
and a cardinal in a dogwood tree.

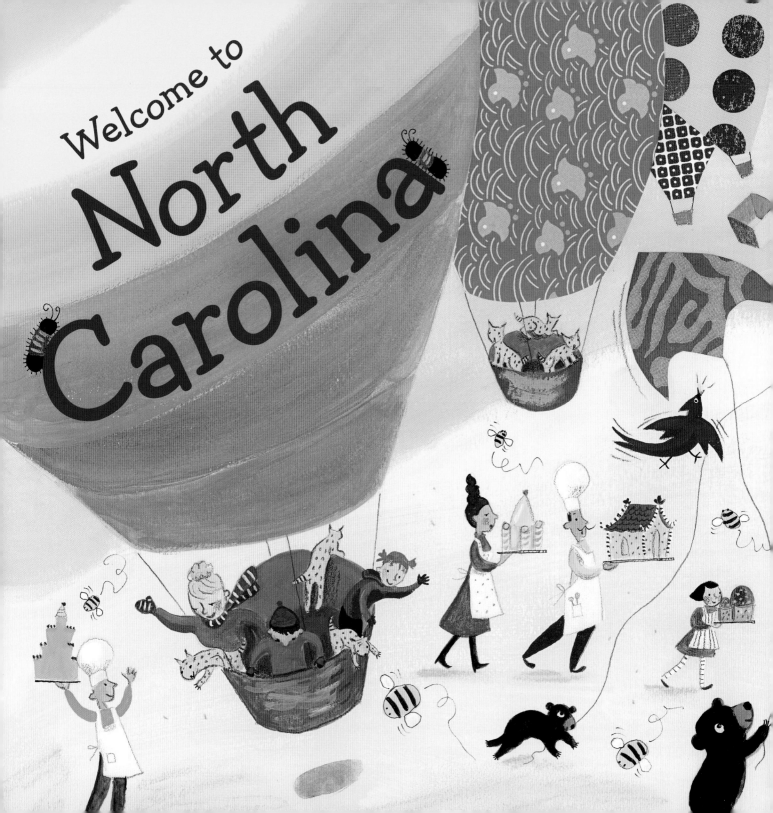

Welcome to
North
Carolina

North Carolina: The Tar Heel State

Capital: Raleigh · **State abbreviation:** NC · **Largest city:** Charlotte · **State bird:** the cardinal · **State flower:** the dogwood · **State tree:** the longleaf pine · **State fruit:** the Scuppernong grape · **State dog:** the Plott hound · **State motto:** "Esse Quam Videri" ("To be, rather than to seem") · **State sports teams:** Panthers (football), Hurricanes (hockey), Bobcats (basketball)

Some Famous North Carolinians:

John Coltrane (1926–1967), born in Hamlet, was a jazz saxophonist and composer who reshaped modern jazz and influenced generations of musicians. A Special Citation from the Pulitzer Prize Board was awarded in Coltrane's honor on the 40th anniversary of his death.

Elizabeth "Liddy" Dole (1936–), born in Salisbury, was elected to the Senate in 2002 as the first female senator for North Carolina. She served in President Reagan's cabinet as secretary of Transportation—the first woman to hold that position.

Roberta Flack (1937–), a Grammy-winning singer, was born in Asheville. She is best known for the singles "The First Time Ever I Saw Your Face," and "Killing Me Softly with His Song," which won the Grammy Record of the Year awards in 1973 and 1974, respectively.

Michael Jordan (1963–) is considered to be "the greatest basketball player of all time." He played college ball for UNC at Chapel Hill. From there he began a long professional career with the Chicago Bulls. He is now a part-owner of the Charlotte Bobcats basketball team.

Dolley Madison (1768–1849) was born in what is now Guilford County. She was married to James Madison, who later became the fourth president of the United States. The enthusiasm and skill she brought to her role as First Lady set the standard for those who followed.

Richard Petty (1937–), born in Level Cross, is one of the greatest NASCAR race car drivers of all time, known for having won the prestigious Winston Cup seven times, and for winning a record 200 races during his career. The Richard Petty Museum is in Randleman.

Carl Sandburg (1878–1967) was a Pulitzer Prize-winning poet and author who lived in Flat Rock from 1945 until his death. He was named "Honorary Ambassador" of North Carolina in 1958. His home is preserved by the National Park Service as the Carl Sandburg Home National Historic Site.

For Tessie, my grandmother, who would have
loved flying "Old Whirlygirl."
—J.S.

STERLING and the distinctive Sterling logo are
registered trademarks of Sterling Publishing Co., Inc

Library of Congress Cataloging-in-Publication Data
Stead, Judy.
The twelve days of Christmas in North Carolina / written and illustrated by Judy Stead.
p. cm.
Summary: On each of the twelve days of her Christmas visit with her cousin Mike, Abby sends her parents a letter describing the history, geography, animals,
and interesting sights of North Carolina. Uses the cumulative pattern of the traditional carol to present amusing state trivia at the end of each letter.
ISBN 978-1-4027-4467-9
[1. North Carolina—Fiction. 2. Letters—Fiction. 3. Christmas—Fiction. 4. Cousins—Fiction.] I. Title.
PZ7.S80855Tw 2009
[E]—dc22   2008043213

Lot#:
8   10   9   7
07/15

Published by Sterling Publishing Co., Inc.
387 Park Avenue South, New York, NY 10016
Text and illustrations © 2009 by Judy Stead
The original illustrations for this book were created using mixed media.
Designed by Kate Moll and Patrice Sheridan.
Distributed in Canada by Sterling Publishing
c/o Canadian Manda Group, 165 Dufferin Street
Toronto, Ontario, Canada M6K 3H6
Distributed in the United Kingdom by GMC Distribution Services
Castle Place, 166 High Street, Lewes, East Sussex, England BN7 1XU
Distributed in Australia by Capricorn Link (Australia) Pty. Ltd.
P.O. Box 704, Windsor, NSW 2756, Australia

Printed in China
All rights reserved

Sterling ISBN 978-1-4027-4467-9

For information about custom editions, special sales, premium and
corporate purchases, please contact Sterling Special Sales
Department at 800-805-5489 or specialsales@sterlingpublishing.com.

Many thanks to the North Carolina Museum of Natural Sciences in Raleigh and
to the Morrison Regional branch of the Public Library of Charlotte and Mecklenburg County
for their invaluable research assistance; and to my powerhouse editorial trio:
Meredith Mundy Wasinger, Andrea Santoro, and NaNá Stoelzle.

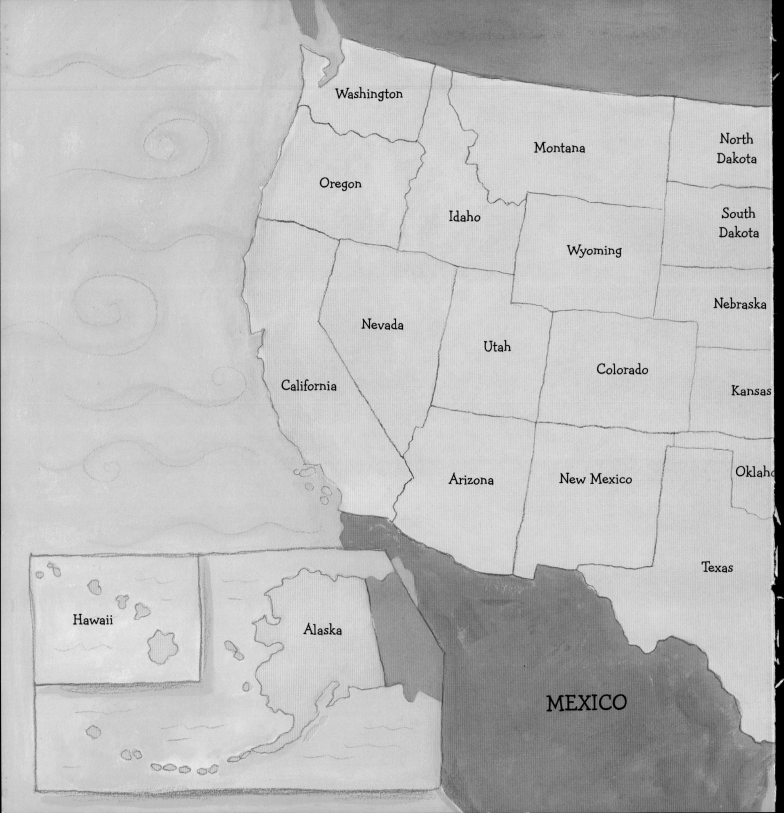